Dear Parents and Educators,

Welcome to Penguin Young Readers! As parents and educators, you know that each child develops at his or her own pace—in terms of speech, critical thinking, and, of course, reading. Penguin Young Readers recognizes this fact. As a result, each Penguin Young Readers book is assigned a traditional easy-to-read level (1–4) as well as a Guided Reading Level (A–P). Both of these systems will help you choose the right book for your child. Please refer to the back of each book for specific leveling information. Penguin Young Readers features esteemed authors and illustrators, stories about favorite characters, fascinating nonfiction, and more!

Tiny Goes Camping

LEVEL **1**

GUIDED READING LEVEL **D**

This book is perfect for an **Emergent Reader** who:
- can read in a left-to-right and top-to-bottom progression;
- can recognize some beginning and ending letter sounds;
- can use picture clues to help tell the story; and
- can understand the basic plot and sequence of simple stories.

Here are some **activities** you can do during and after reading this book:
- Story Map: A story map is a visual organizer that helps the reader understand what happens in a story. On a separate sheet of paper, create a story map of this story. The map should include the beginning (who are the characters and what will they be doing?), middle (what are the characters doing after the story gets started?), and ending (how does the story end?).
- Word Repetition: Reread the story and count how many times you read the following words: need, too, camp. On a separate sheet of paper, work with the child to write a new sentence for each word.

Remember, sharing the love of reading with a child is the best gift you can give!

—Bonnie Bader, EdM
   Penguin Young Readers program

WITHDRAWN

*Penguin Young Readers are leveled by independent reviewers applying the standards developed by Irene Fountas and Gay Su Pinnell in *Matching Books to Readers: Using Leveled Books in Guided Reading*, Heinemann, 1999.

For Jameson—CM

To Juan and Jim, my special brothers
in Christ . . . It is an incredible privilege to walk
on the road of life with you! NORTH!—RD

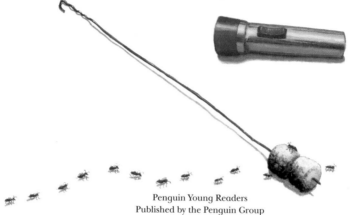

Penguin Young Readers
Published by the Penguin Group
Penguin Group (USA) Inc., 375 Hudson Street, New York, New York 10014, USA
Penguin Group (Canada), 90 Eglinton Avenue East, Suite 700, Toronto, Ontario M4P 2Y3, Canada
(a division of Pearson Penguin Canada Inc.)
Penguin Books Ltd, 80 Strand, London WC2R 0RL, England
Penguin Ireland, 25 St Stephen's Green, Dublin 2, Ireland (a division of Penguin Books Ltd)
Penguin Group (Australia), 707 Collins Street, Melbourne, Victoria 3008, Australia
(a division of Pearson Australia Group Pty Ltd)
Penguin Books India Pvt Ltd, 11 Community Centre, Panchsheel Park, New Delhi—110 017, India
Penguin Group (NZ), 67 Apollo Drive, Rosedale, Auckland 0632, New Zealand
(a division of Pearson New Zealand Ltd)
Penguin Books (South Africa), Rosebank Office Park, 181 Jan Smuts Avenue,
Parktown North 2193, South Africa
Penguin China, B7 Jiaming Center, 27 East Third Ring Road North,
Chaoyang District, Beijing 100020, China

Penguin Books Ltd, Registered Offices: 80 Strand, London WC2R 0RL, England

Text copyright © 2006 by Cari Meister. Illustrations copyright © 2006 by Rich Davis. All rights reserved.
First published in 2006 by Viking and in 2007 by Puffin Books, imprints of Penguin Group (USA) Inc.
Published in 2013 by Penguin Young Readers, an imprint of Penguin Group (USA) Inc.,
345 Hudson Street, New York, New York 10014. Manufactured in China.

The Library of Congress has cataloged the Viking edition
under the following Control Number: 2005022822

ISBN 978-0-14-056741-0   10

Tiny Goes Camping

by Cari Meister
illustrated by Rich Davis

Penguin Young Readers
An Imprint of Penguin Group (USA) Inc.

This is my dog.

His name is Tiny.

Tiny loves to camp.

I do, too.

We need to pack.

We need a tent.

We need a flashlight.

We need food.

Oh, Tiny!
That is too
much food!

Where can we camp?

Not here.

Too many rocks.

Not here.

Too many sticks.

Tiny finds a good spot.

Good dog, Tiny!

We put up the tent.

We eat camp food.

We sing a camp song.

Tiny spots something.

What is it, Tiny?

A frog!

Look, Tiny!

Fireflies!

We chase them.

We catch them.

We put them in a jar.

Now we have a night-light.

Time for bed, Tiny.

28

Oh no!

The tent is too small.

POP!

Oh no!

That's okay.

Now we can see the stars.

Good night, Tiny.

Sweet dreams.